Peter Nickl   Binette Schroeder

Ra ta ta tam

The strange story of a little engine

Translated from the German by Michael Bullock

JONATHAN CAPE THIRTY BEDFORD

For
Mathias
and
Julia

Matthew Tiny was a little man, a tiny little man, not quite as small as Tom Thumb, a bit bigger than the Cornish pixies, almost as big as you children. And he loved railway engines so much that the bigger people in his town thought it a bit odd. Perhaps he was odd. But above all, Matthew Tiny was very, very clever. He solved the most difficult arithmetic problems with his left hand, and at the same time he built the most extraordinary things with his right. He was famous in his town as the inventor of the unique underwater-paddle-steamer and the strange pedal-propelled-bicycle-balloon.

But what he liked best of all were railway engines. He often used to slip into the big factory on the outskirts of the town and sit on the roof of an engine. Then he dreamed of being an engine driver and travelling around the world. He dreamed of railway lines and level crossings, signals and points and the everlasting ratatatam, ratatatam, ratatatam.

But the workmen used to come along and shoo him away. "Beat it, Tiny," they shouted. "Trot along on your own two feet."

Matthew Tiny climbed down and went off grumbling to himself, "I've had enough of this. I must have an engine. I'll build one for myself."

And what do you think he did? Day after day he borrowed a few spare parts from the factory and in a couple of weeks there was a tiny little engine in the factory yard, snow white and as pretty as a picture.

The workmen were filled with admiration and the big engines rumbled in amazement.

"What a pretty little engine," said the factory owner, rubbing his hands. "That's for me."

"No, it belongs to me!" cried Matthew Tiny.

"Oh no, little fellow," smiled the factory owner. "Everything here belongs to the factory."

"No, it belongs to me!" yelled Matthew Tiny. "I invented it. I made it, not you, Fat Face."

That was too much for the factory owner. "Get out," he yelled. "Get out at once."

Matthew Tiny went. Soon after that, he left the town in one of his strange vehicles. "I'm going to where people are friendly," he said before leaving.

Next morning at breakfast the factory owner said to his wife, "It's such a pretty little thing, darling, let's put it in our garden."

And when the little railway engine was standing in her beautiful garden, the factory owner's wife said, "Yes, it's as pretty as a poem."

"Silly goose," chugged the little engine when it heard this. Then it jumped down off its pedestal and chased the factory owner's wife over the flower beds.

"Help, help! The world is coming to an end," screamed the factory owner's wife in horror. But suddenly there was a violent crash, the iron gate to the garden was smashed open and the little engine made off down the road.

"Right, that's the first step," it whistled, and trundled gaily off across the countryside.

It wasn't long before it came to a wide wilderness. "Ratatatam," it groaned. "Ratatatam. Now I'm tired, soon I won't be able to go at all."

The little engine grew sad. Dark night fell and the big, white moon rose in the sky.

"Where are you going?" hooted an owl from its tree.

"I'm looking for my little Matthew Tiny," lamented the railway engine. The owl answered with a riddle:

> Tiny is near and Tiny is far.
> He's on his way to the evening star,
> And he who seeks him in vain today
> To the depths of the earth must make his way.

"Stuff and nonsense," hissed the little engine and clattered off.

Ratatatam, Ratatatam, Ratatatam, Ratatatam, Ratatatam, Ratatatam, Ratatatam, Ratatatam.

Next morning it came to the outskirts of a big city. The city was as black as if blackness had rained down on it from the sky during the night.

Full of curiosity, the little engine trundled into the black city. There it found a man leaning against a tree singing:

> Here we live in a coal mine town,
> Day in day out the same old round,
> Shovelling for all we're worth
> Black gold from the deepest depths of the earth.

"Oh," chugged the little engine delightedly, "gold!" And the man leaning against the tree jumped aboard and went down with the engine into the depths of the earth.

They didn't find any gold. They found coal, and they found work, and they both turned quite black with it.

"How long are you going to go on doing this?" the little engine asked one day.

"For ever," said the man. "It's my job."

"Well, it's not my job," said the engine, coughing coal dust out of its funnel, and trundled off, black as it was, out of the city.

"Otherwise I'll never find Tiny," it whistled to itself.

"Stay here," shouted the man. "You belong to me. You belong in the coal mine." But the engine didn't even hear him any more. It was already travelling across green meadows.

But suddenly it saw huge clouds of smoke rising from every corner of the city. "They're starting up the railway engines," it cried. "They're going to chase me."

And that was quite true. Enormous black engines were already thundering along all the tracks.

The air shook and boomed. "I must get away. I must get away. Where can I go? Where can I go?" hissed the little engine.

The monsters were coming closer and closer.

"They'll catch me. They'll catch me. Oh heavens, they'll catch me," the little engine groaned, completely out of breath and giving up all hope.

Then a great rain cloud came up overhead, turning everything dark. There was thunder and lightning and a terrible storm of rain splattered down on the earth.

Then the storm passed. The sun shone again and our little engine, once more beautifully white, jumped off the rails and called out to the big black railway engines, "Quick! Hurry! The little black engine just went round that corner. You'll catch it if you hurry."

The big black engines raced past the little white engine like a flock of wet ravens. But the little engine got back on to the track and trundled along behind them - ratatatam - thinking to itself, if I keep behind them they'll never catch me.

And the little engine was right. It never saw or heard of its pursuers again. Its way led high up into the mountains. Everywhere was glistening snow. It came to a small village inhabited by little people with friendly faces.

"End of the line," whistled the engine. "I'm staying here." And it was just about to blow off steam when a tiny little man ran down the mountainside with open arms.

People say that when the little white engine saw
Matthew Tiny such an enormous cloud of smoke rose
from its funnel that the whole village was buried in
fog for three days and three nights.

Many years have passed since then,
and today the little engine is still
going up and down the mountain day after day
carrying Matthew Tiny and his friends.

Ratatatam, Ratatatam, Ratatatam, Ratatatam, Ratatatam, Ratatatam.

By the same authors
THE CROCODILE

First published in Great Britain 1974
Reprinted 1975, 1978, 1983
Text and illustrations © 1973 by Nord-Süd Verlag, Mönchaltorf and Hamburg
Translation © 1974 by Jonathan Cape Ltd
Printed in Germany by Druckerei Uhl, Radolfzell
Jonathan Cape Ltd., 30 Bedford Square, London WC1

ISBN 0 224 00974 5